ACT NORMAL

AND DON'T TELL ANYONE ABOUT THE

ZOMBIE
ROBOTS

Christian Darkin

CHAPTER 1

This is a story about toys and phones and a game called, "Zombie Robots". There are also some real zombie robots, but they come in later.

It's also a story about two problems.

The first problem is that bedrooms are often very untidy. There are often lots of toys and things lying around. Underneath beds is especially bad because that's where all the old things and the broken things and the things you don't use anymore go, and some pretty scary things can happen down there if you don't watch out.

The second problem is that grown-ups spend far too much time playing on their phones.

People in this story:

Me: I am Jenny. I try to keep things under control, but sometimes it is very difficult. I am good at working things out, so I often know that things are going to get out of control before they do. That makes it a little bit easier to stop them, but only a little bit.

Adam: Adam is my Brother. He likes things to get out of control. He also likes robots and zombie robots are his favourite kind of robots. He is good at video games and throwing things.

Dad: When things get broken, some people really mind a lot. Dad doesn't mind too much because he is used to it in our house. This is lucky because in this story, the whole town gets broken, and having someone around who doesn't get too upset makes it easier to fix things.

CHAPTER 2

My brother, Adam was a bit sad. This was because he wanted to run away from a monster, but the monster was not chasing him.

We were at Kidsworld, which is a very big room, full of climbing frames and mazes and slides, and lots of children who run about and shout a lot. There is even a big ball pit at the bottom of one of the slides, so when you slide down, you get completely covered in balls.

Normally, Dad is the monster, and he chases us around Kidsworld. It is better than when he does it at home, because at Kidsworld, we can climb up into the maze. Dad is really slow at the maze because it has small holes that he can't fit through.

Also, in Kidsworld there are no things made of glass, and you are allowed to jump on EVERYTHING.

Today, Dad was not being the monster. Today, Dad had got his new phone and he was sitting at a table, drinking coffee and putting apps onto it.

Today, Adam and I had to be our own monsters and chase each other.

I am a very clever monster, and I can see which bit of the maze Adam is going to come out of. I get there first and grab him so he screams.

Adam is a very fast monster, and he is a loud monster. He also never ever stops, so he is good at catching me.

We chased each other round and round and up and down. I almost caught him lots of times, but he just ran past and laughed.

In the end, I saw him get onto a long, curly slide, so I ran up the slide to catch him. I did catch him but he was going very fast and we both fell into the ball pit and bumped.

We went to tell Dad and find out whose fault it was.

Dad was not putting apps onto his new phone. Dad was playing a game on his phone! The game was all about zombie robots.

My brother and I told Dad what had happened. Dad carried on playing "Zombie Robots".

My brother told Dad it was my fault that we had bumped because I had climbed up the slide.

I told Dad it was my brother's fault because he was not supposed to be the monster. He was supposed to be running away, not hitting me.

Dad said, "Just play nicely," which was not an answer. Then he kept on playing "Zombie Robots".

In the end, we had to both cry and then he put his phone down and said he would be the monster.

He chased us round the whole maze and roared really loudly. Then we got cake.

When Dad was standing waiting to get the cake, I looked around at all the grown-ups in Kidsworld, and do you know what I saw?

Every single one of them was playing "Zombie Robots" on their phones! None of them were watching what their kids were doing, and none of them were being monsters.

They were just staring at their phones and pressing buttons.

When we got home, I decided to find out just what was going on...

CHAPTER 3

I knew Dad put his old phone under his bed
when he got the new one. I sent Adam to
get it because it is not nice under there.

There are some old socks which probably
have toenails in them, and two or three
pairs of pants with holes in. There are also
a lot of different kinds of dirt and dust and
some of it might be alive.

Adam crawled under and came out with 5 old phones, and 7 different kinds of wires to plug into them. He also came out with a dead pot plant and a book about parrots. We took the phones and wires to my room.

Dad's old phone worked when we plugged it in and putting "Zombie Robots" onto it was easy because Dad's password is "Jenny".

That is easy to remember because it is my
name. And his bank pin number is 0612.

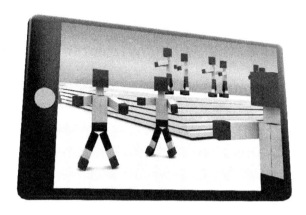

"Zombie Robots" is a game where you have
to shoot all the zombie robots with a
special anti-zombie robot gun. When I shot
them, they blew up into lots of little bits.

But then there was a problem because all
the other zombie robots just stuck all the
bits back together to make more zombie
robots.

It was fun to start with but, then they started taking bits from cars and houses and building them into zombie robots too. Soon, there were so many zombie robots that I couldn't shoot them fast enough and they just kept getting closer and closer and then they got me.

That is what is wrong with the game.

After a while, I got bored with playing "Zombie Robots", and I gave it to Adam.

He was much better at shooting zombie robots than me, and he found out that if you got to the end of a level (that means you killed all the zombie robots which is very hard to do) then a really big zombie robot came in. If you killed that one, there was a reset button you could press.

When Adam pressed the reset button, all the zombie robots stopped attacking him, and started taking themselves to pieces to build back into all the cars and houses and things they had been made out of.

Then it all started again. The only way you could stop the zombie robots forever was to shoot them all AND the big one at the end of the level, and then keep doing that for EVERY SINGLE LEVEL. There were about 20 levels and each one was harder than the last one.

While Adam played, I decided to see what was under my bed. There were lots of toys which I had forgotten all about.

There was a doll baby who used to waggle her legs to crawl around (but not since I dropped her and some of the wires came out of her nose). There was a remote controlled caterpillar without a control, and there were a lot of kits which I had only got around to making half of.

When Adam saw all the toys, he said they looked like the bits in "Zombie Robots". He asked me to make a real toy zombie robot for him.

I really, really should have said, "No," but I didn't.

I got the doll and stuck it to the caterpillar and put some bits from the kits all together onto it so that it looked like a real zombie robot. Then I got all the wires from the doll's nose and I twisted them all up with the wires from the caterpillar.

It looked a bit messy, but Adam loved it. He gave me Dad's old phone and said, "Put this on it. Then it can have zombie robots on it."

I stuck the phone on the front, and I found one of Dad's wires that let me plug the phone into the doll.

Adam was laughing a lot. He said, "It's a real zombie robot!" and we went to get his Nerf gun to fire at it.

Then Dad called us for tea.

That was when I got the first idea that something bad had happened, because when we got back, the zombie robot was gone...

CHAPTER 1

We couldn't find the zombie robot anywhere, but both our rooms are a bit messy, so I thought it was probably somewhere in the mess.

I found out what had really happened when I woke up in the night.

I heard a whizzing, whirring sound which I thought was part of my dream (my dream was about clockwork ducks). Then I opened my eyes and the sound did not stop like dreams do.

Also, there was a flashing light coming from under my bed. I looked under, and do you know what I saw?

My zombie robot was there, and I couldn't believe my eyes. It was moving about on its own!

The phone was playing a game of "Zombie Robots" but the caterpillar and the doll's arms were all moving about at the same time as the zombie robots in the game. It was running about, playing the game under the bed!

I watched what it was doing. First, it got all of my old toys from under the bed and put them in a big pile.

It picked up each bit of each toy and held it in front of the phone's camera. It took a photo of each piece.

Then, it wriggled its way over to the door, and went out.

After 2 or 3 minutes, it came back in. It was dragging all the old army toys from under Adam's bed.

Slowly, it picked up each bit of each toy, and held it in front of the camera. Then the zombie robot sorted all the bits of toys into 4 piles.

I didn't like the look of this at all. Toys were not supposed to work all on their own, except in films.

The next thing the zombie robot did was to go and get Dad's 4 other old mobile phones and put one on each pile of toy bits.

Then it started to stick and clip and twist wires together in each pile. It was turning all the old toys from under our beds, and all the old phones from under Dad's bed into more zombie robots!

I was a bit tired, but I decided this was bad, and that it was time for it to stop.

I put my hand slowly under the bed and pulled out the little zombie robot. It wriggled a bit, but I held it by one of the doll's arms and I turned off the phone.

Then I went back to sleep.

In the morning, Adam woke me up for school. I looked under the bed, and do you know what I found?

Nothing.

The zombie robot was gone. I must have not done a very good job in turning it off.

Not only that, but the 4 piles of toy bits and Dad's 4 other old phones were gone as well...

CHAPTER 5

At breakfast time, I didn't say anything about the zombie robot (which was probably now 5 zombie robots). I just acted normal.

It was easy, because Dad was playing "Zombie Robots" on his new phone again. Dad hadn't got round to making breakfast, so I got some chocolate muddy puffs for us.

We only usually have them for special treats, but I think if you have to make your own breakfast, you get to decide what it is.

If Dad wanted to decide, then he had to stop playing on his phone first. He didn't stop. He just looked up and made a, "Hmmm..." noise which was actually a bit like a zombie.

In the car, on the way to school, Adam and I played counting. We counted the number of people we saw playing "Zombie Robots" on their phones.

There were 126 (but I think my brother counted some people twice). I think "Zombie Robots" must be an addictive game.

Addictive means you can't stop playing it even if you want to. People say, "It's addictive!" as if that is a bad thing, but they smile when they say it, and then they keep playing it, so I don't know.

We saw people playing it at bus stops and teachers playing it in the playground. We even saw some people playing it in their cars and that is definitely very bad.

I'm actually getting a bit worried about the grown-ups because, "Zombie Robots" sort of turns everyone who plays it into zombie robots. They don't talk to you or look at you or do anything at all except walk around staring at their screens.

I'm also getting a bit worried about the real toy zombie robots I made because I don't know where they are or what they're doing.

In maths, the teacher, Mrs. Gubbins was secretly playing on her phone, so I did some adding up of my own.

I started by writing down what I knew:

- It took my zombie robot one night to make 4 new zombie robots from the toys under our beds.

- All those robots have escaped.

- All the children I know have broken toys under their beds.

- All the grown-ups have old phones under their beds.

Then I asked myself this question: How many zombie robots would there be tomorrow?

There are probably 5 now, so each of those 5 could make 4 more by the end of today. That means 5x4=20 plus the 5 that were there already = 25.

Then tonight, those 25 would each make 4 more, so tomorrow morning there would be 25x4=100 plus 25 =125.

Then by tomorrow evening there would be 125x4+125=625.

I had to get a calculator to work out how many there would be by Saturday, and do you know what the answer was?

CHAPTER 6

48,828,125

That's nearly 49 million.

By school time on Monday, there would be 30,517,578,125. That's a really big number.

There are 7,000,000,000 (7 billion) people on Earth so that means each person would have more than 4 zombie robots – and that was just on Monday!

And that would make things very hard for everyone.

When we got home, Adam and I searched everywhere for the zombie robots. They were not anywhere in the house. Also, they were not in the garden.

We looked in the wood, and I thought I saw one of them – but it might just have been one of the little dinosaurs that live in the wood (there are little dinosaurs in the wood because of something I did by mistake a few weeks ago, but that is in another story).

I sent an email to everybody from my class:

Dear Everybody,

Please look under your beds tonight, and if you see any zombie robots please catch them.

PS: Please don't have nightmares about zombie robots coming out from under your bed and taking over the world because it probably won't happen.

PPS: Just in case it does happen, it might be a good plan to tidy your bedrooms so that they can't make more zombie robots out of your toys while you're asleep.

Love, Jenny.

I could see this all getting out of control very quickly, but on the way to school the next day, we didn't see any zombie robots at all.

There were even more grown-ups acting like zombie robots and staring at their screens, but no real toy zombie robots at all.

I thought it might all be OK after all, but I was wrong...

CHAPTER 7

I didn't see any zombie robots all morning.
There weren't even any at lunchtime.

I remembered that the only one I had ever
seen was the one I made, and I thought
maybe it had just taken all the bits and
then run out of power before it got to make
more zombie robots. Or maybe, it wasn't
trying to make more zombie robots at all.
Maybe it was just tidying up our bedrooms
for us. Or maybe I had dreamed it.

But then we had science in the afternoon. I got to the science room early because I like doing experiments, but when I opened the door, I saw something very bad.

My zombie robot was there, in the middle of the room – the first ever real toy zombie robot. It had got all the science things out of all the cupboards and it was building something on one of the desks.

What it was building was very definitely
another zombie robot – a very sciency one!

It hadn't finished, so I ran over, grabbed
the first ever real toy zombie robot and
stuffed it into my school bag. I could feel
it wriggling about in there, but it couldn't
get out because I shut the bag tight.

I had to find Adam.

It didn't take long. He was in his classroom with everyone else. They were all looking out of the window.

"Look," said Adam, "Zombie robots!" I couldn't believe what I was seeing. Out of the window we could see over the school wall and out into the town. There were zombie robots everywhere!

All the old and broken toys from all the children of the town and all the old phones of all the grown-ups had been taken to bits and turned into strange robots, and they were rolling, walking, wriggling and jumping through the town looking for more things to turn into more zombie robots.

As I watched, I saw one climb up the school wall, and sit on the top, looking around the playground. It had lots and lots of action-man legs, a teddy bear body and an old laptop with a broken screen. It looked like a spider with a screen.

Then, after it, lots of tiny Hexbug robots all crawled up too. Each one had a toy soldier stuck to it. All the robots in the town were moving towards the school.

The teachers hadn't even noticed what was happening. They were all playing "Zombie Robots" on their phones and they weren't even looking up!

"Quick!" I said, "Come with me!" and we all ran down to the playground. We started pushing the zombie robots back over the school wall as fast as we could.

The little Hexbug robots had got over, and the soldiers were firing little stones at our ankles. We chased them round and round the playground, and threw them back over the wall. But there were so many zombie

robots, it was very hard to keep them out.

Then, Adam picked up a chair and threw it

over the wall at the robots (Adam can

throw anything a really long way).

It hit one of the zombie robots and

knocked it into a car. But the robot didn't

stop, it just took the chair in one hand (it

had three hands). Then it pulled the engine

out of the car and turned the chair and the

engine into another, bigger robot!

After a second, the car's sat-nav (which was stuck on the top of the new robot) turned itself on, loaded up the "Zombie Robots" game and started playing.

That made the new robot come to life. The engine started, and it rolled towards the school.

This was bad.

Also, I noticed that while we were stopping the robots coming over the wall, the school gates at the other end of the playground were wide open.

I said, "Come on. We have to shut the school gates!" Everybody ran to the gates and started pulling them shut.

The zombie robots had seen the gates too now, and they were coming towards them.

Suddenly, Dad's car came around the corner very fast. There were zombie robots hanging onto it. The car crashed through the gates and skidded to a stop.

Dad got out and helped us shut the gate, and we threw the robots that were hanging onto it back over the wall.

"It's OK," said Dad, "I've called the army."

CHAPTER 8

Calling the army is something you only do when things are really, really bad. We have only had to call the army 6 or 7 times in my whole life!

We all ran back into the school, locked the doors and waited for the army. By now, we could see that the zombie Robots were not just using toys and phones. They had taken all the computers out of the shops and they were making more robots out of bits of cars, and lampposts, and fences, and even houses.

There was one robot being built by about 20 other little ones. It had a truck for wheels, two big digger arms and on its head was the whole roof of a house.

Its tummy had a cinema screen on it, and we could see "Zombie Robots" was being loaded up on it. It was just like the giant robots at the end of each level of the game.

The army arrived. They were very loud. They had tanks and trucks and helicopters.

Adam loves it when the army arrives, and he and his friends all clapped and cheered.

Then the army started fighting the zombie robots. They shot some of them, and they used their tanks to run over some others and squash them.

It was very noisy and lots of bits of the town were broken very quickly, but it didn't take very long before things got worse.

The robots that got broken fixed

themselves very quickly. Then they started

taking the trucks and the tanks and the

helicopters to bits and making them all into

giant zombie robots.

They built them as tall as buildings and used the army's guns and tanks and even pieces of furniture and walls from houses that had been pulled down.

That was when the army ran away.

So now, instead of a few little toy zombie robots, we had an army of giant zombie robots. Things had not gone quite as well as I had hoped.

That's when I made a plan. It was a good plan, but it needed Dad and Adam to do some very hard things very quickly...

CHAPTER 9

I said, "Dad, you have to phone the army and tell them to switch off the Internet when I say so."

Then I got the first ever real toy zombie robot out of my school bag. It was still wriggling around a lot and it took 4 of us to hold it down.

"Now Adam," I said, "You have to play 'Zombie Robots'. You have to play it so well that you beat the big robots on every single level of the game."

Do you remember when Adam first played "Zombie Robots" and he was very good at it? Do you remember that he beat all the robots until he got to a big robot at the end of the level, and that when he beat that, he got a reset button to make the robots build everything back together again?

And remember you could only really stop them forever by beating every single level in the whole game?

Well, that is what Adam had to do now. We all held the first ever real toy zombie robot down, and Adam played, and played, and played.

He beat one level of zombie robots and then he beat another level. Then he lost and had to start again, but still he kept on playing.

He beat more and more levels of zombie robots until his fingers were so tired he could hardly press the screen. He played until he never wanted to see another computer game ever again.

Dad called the army and they got ready to turn off the Internet.

By now, the real giant army zombie robots were crashing through the school walls, and hammering on the doors. They were taking the whole town to bits and making more and more real giant robots. The windows were shaking and the noise was very, very loud. They were getting closer, and closer, and closer.

Then Adam said, "Yes!" He had beaten all the levels of "Zombie Robots" and he had found a giant reset button.

I told him to press the button, and at the same time, I told Dad to tell the army to switch off the Internet.

Suddenly everything stopped. All the zombie robots outside were being told what to do by the "Zombie Robots" game on the Internet. Now, the Internet was turned off, none of the zombie robots knew what to do.

The only thing they could do was follow what the first real toy zombie robot did.

Now, Adam had beaten the last level of the game on the first ever real toy zombie robot and pressed the reset button...

CHAPTER 10

Slowly, all the zombie robots turned around and started to walk and crawl and roll and wiggle and fly (remember; some of them were made from helicopters) back into town.

Slowly, one by one, they began to take themselves to pieces. The little robots jumped onto the big ones and unscrewed and unstuck and unplugged pieces and slowly, they dragged each piece back to where they had got it from.

Slowly, the robots re-built all the things they had broken, and slowly, they put the town back together.

Once they'd finished, and the very last robot had taken itself completely to bits, I told Dad that the army could turn the Internet back on again.

The zombie robots didn't get everything exactly as it had been before.

Some of the cars got the wrong coloured doors, and some of the houses didn't have exactly the same rooms as they had before.

A very small house ended up with the roof from a very big house. One family living in a tiny flat on the 13th floor of a tower block opened their hall cupboard to find that it lead into a huge mansion built on the side of the block.

One row of houses were re-built with just one tiny room on each floor.

Some of the houses had wheels, and some of the cars had basements.

Some of the houses were made of furniture, and some of the furniture was made of houses.

But, everyone eventually got sorted out, and things went sort of back to normal.

The funny thing was, though, that for a whole day, there was no Internet. The grown-ups couldn't check their email, or update Facebook, or play on their phones.

All the grown-ups and the children came out to play together, and went for walks outside, and had picnics in the park while they watched the giant zombie robots rebuilding their houses.

When it was time for the Internet to go back on, the first thing Dad did was switch on his phone. I thought he was going to play "Zombie Robots" but he wasn't.

"I'm going to delete all the games on my phone," he said to me and Adam, "But you'd better start running. Because then I'm going to be a monster!"

And the monster chased us around for the rest of the day.

The end.

Things to do:

- If you liked this book, why not have a go at writing a review on Amazon?

- Please tell your friends on Facebook and in real life.

- There are lots of other "Act Normal" books. Why not just type "Act Normal" into Amazon and see what you can find?

- If you'd like the author, Christian Darkin to come and visit your school, you can get all the details at https://christiandarkin.wordpress.com/.

The illustrations are by the author, but use some elements for which I'd like to credit and thank: www.obsidiandawn.com, kuschelirmel-stock, and waywardgal

Story and illustrations by © Christian Darkin

Act Normal and read more...

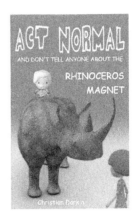

CPSIA information can be obtained
at www.ICGtesting.com
Printed in the USA
LVOW04s0558210516

489255LV00029B/654/P

9 781505 515978